Look Out, Duggy Dog!

Brian Ball

Illustrated by
Lesley Smith

Hamish Hamilton
London

First published in Great Britain 1985
by Hamish Hamilton Children's Books
Garden House 57–59 Long Acre London WC2E 9JZ
Text copyright © 1985 by Brian Ball
Illustrations copyright © 1985 by Lesley Smith

July 11th

British Library Cataloguing in Publication Data
Ball, Brian, 1932——
Look out, Duggy Dog.——(Cartwheels)
I. Title   II. Smith, Lesley   III. Series
823'.914[J]   PZ7

ISBN 0–241–11597–3

Colour separations by Anglia Reproductions
Typeset by Katerprint Co. Ltd, Oxford
Printed in Great Britain by
Blantyre Printing and Binding Ltd
London and Glasgow

Duggy Dog was snoozing in the garden.
The flies were buzzing all around and the
birds were chirping in the trees.

A lovely smell came from Mrs Smith's
kitchen. Duggy Dog's nose twitched.
His tail wagged.

"I know that smell," he said. "Sausage rolls! Yummy!" Duggy Dog followed the smell into the kitchen.

Mrs Smith pointed to the door.

"Uh-oh," said Duggy Dog. "I know. Out!"

He went out of the back door. He went through the back garden and out onto the Big Field to call for his friends.

First, he went to Floss's house. She
liked to play chase.

Floss was sitting next to a pram,
looking very important.

"Go away," said Floss.

"Don't you want to play chase on the
Big Field?" asked Duggy Dog.

"No," said Floss. "We have got a new baby and I am looking after it. Now go away."

So Duggy Dog ran to Minty's house. Minty liked playing chase too, but she did not look pleased to see Duggy Dog.

"Come and play chase, Minty!" called
Duggy Dog.

"No. I am staying at home," said Minty.
"There is a new dog on the Big Field.
He is big and nasty. He has long, sharp
teeth. He told me to keep away."

Minty was too scared to come out to play so Duggy Dog went to call for little Jasper.

Little Jasper was hiding in the bushes.
"Who is that?" he yelped.
"Me," said Duggy Dog. "Come and play chase!"

But little Jasper was too scared to come out of the bushes. The nasty dog had told him to keep off the Big Field too.

Duggy Dog was fed up.

"If you are not coming to play then I am going home for a sausage roll," he said.

Duggy Dog dashed back over the Big
Field to his own house.

Duggy Dog sat down on the step.

The flies were still buzzing all around.

One fly buzzed into the yellow watering-can.

Why had it gone in there?

16

Duggy Dog looked inside. He asked
the fly what it was doing.

"I'm stuck," said the fly. "I'm trying
to find a way out!"

Duggy Dog laughed. What a silly fly,
to get stuck in a watering-can!

Around and around buzzed the fly
until it found the spout.

"I've found the way out now," it said,
as it flew up the spout. "Good-bye!"

Then Duggy Dog tried to get his head
out of the watering-can. But he was
stuck, too!

The fly buzzed back.

"You had better hurry, Duggy Dog,"
it said. "There is a big nasty dog with
long, sharp teeth, coming this way."

"Uh-oh . . ." said Duggy Dog.

The fly buzzed away but Duggy Dog didn't hear it go. He was too busy trying to get his head out of the watering-can before the big nasty dog came.

"The fly went up the spout," said
Duggy Dog. "Maybe I could get out that
way too."

He looked up the spout of the
watering-can.

And there, looking back at him, was
the big nasty dog, with long, sharp teeth!

"Wuff!" growled Duggy Dog. "Wuff-wuff! What do you want?"

The big dog did not answer.

Duggy Dog banged the watering-can on the grass as hard as he could. He banged it on the bushes. He banged it on the fence.

Then he banged it on the big nasty dog. . .

"*Helllpppp!*" the big dog wailed.
"A horrible Yellow Thing is after me!"
"Where?" said Duggy Dog. "What
Yellow Thing?"
But the big dog was running away as fast
as he could go.

24

"I am not coming here any more," he
yelped. "Not where the horrible Yellow
Thing lives! I will never come near the
Big Field again."

Duggy Dog did not hear what the big dog was saying. He was still trying to shake off the yellow watering-can.

Then Minty and little Jasper came running up. They stopped and stared in amazement.

Just then, Duggy Dog gave the yellow watering-can an extra-strong shake.

Off it flew!

"Oh, it is you, Duggy Dog!" cried
Minty and Jasper.

Duggy Dog looked surprised. The
big nasty dog had gone.

"You scared him away," Minty said.

"You are clever, Duggy Dog," said
Jasper.

Duggy Dog smiled a doggy smile.

"Any time," he told his friends.

Little Jasper and Minty went off to play
chase on the Big Field, now it was safe
again, but Duggy Dog could smell a lovely
smell coming from Mrs Smith's kitchen.

Mrs Smith was putting something
into his dish.

"Come on!" cried Minty and little Jasper.

"I won't be long," said Duggy Dog. "Just as long as it takes to eat a sausage roll," he said.

And it didn't take long at all.